HUNGERFATE

THE KIDNAPPING OF JASON SMITH

ERIC REESE

A book must be the axe for the frozen sea within us.

FRANZ KAFKA

CONTENTS

When one talked about survival, the first thing that come into the minds of the people was surviving in a forest, in a mountainous region, or at sea. But what most didn't expect was that survival, in truth, meant the ability for one to live in such situations that no one else could ever consider or hope of being in. Survival, in a nutshell, means that someone lived in a place without the natural resources that one would find in a comfortable house or a comfortable home. That is what it meant to survive. And that is what the young boy by the name of Jason Smith did.

Jason was merely sixteen and didn't think of himself as anyone special. He was just a simple boy with some a few friends living in a simple house without a worry in the world. Sure, he'd cry with everyone when someone inside of his family died and he'd laugh with everyone when there was a time to laugh, but he would not shed a single tear or give a single glance if someone suddenly jumped up and screamed that there was an outbreak of dancing monkeys in some random city, for it most certainly didn't concern him at all.

But when things went down a certain way, and when things didn't go his way, there was nothing he could do except for pray, pray that there was someone or something that would perhaps save him.

'Please give me strength.' He thought as he took deep breaths. *'Please give me strength. Please give me strength.'*

And the reason why he was doing such a thing was that he was currently tied over on the chair, alone, inside of a dark room with nowhere to go. He didn't know what he had to do, but he knew that if he didn't have the strength, then no one could save him and he'd definitely be alone in this world of complete and utter pain and agony. Yes, that was the case, he just couldn't do things all by himself.

His hands and legs were bound by some dirty rags that Jason couldn't believe were still in use. He could smell the dirty and disgusting pieces of filth still inside of the rags, and he could still smell whatever it was previously used for. He knew for a fact that if the rag was used against his mouth and his nose, he would pass out, but they were at least merciful enough to leave his face uncovered, yet put a simple ball-gag inside of his mouth. He knew that he was in a rock and a hard place and if he didn't do something, he was, for sure, going to die. But first, he needed to know where he was, why he was kidnapped, and who in their right minds would kidnap someone as destructive and as useless as him. Right, there was utterly no one that would give a care about him, no one, and that was what was making him cry out in utter pain and agony.

And in that moment of weakness, he realized something. He realized the words of his Grandfather, his dear old Grandfather who always told him everything he needed to know. His dear old Grandfather who always wanted him to be strong. Jason knew that his Grandfather was dead and he was not going to be able to see him succeed anymore, but he had left behind a very, very important lesson.

'Never be dependent on Someone, my Grandson. Never.'

That was his lesson. His Grandfather always wanted him to be an independent man and grow up to be perhaps the greatest of all the men that were out there, that was the only way that he could be great, the only way that he could be perfect. 'And always remain strong. Because if you aren't strong, then no one will be strong for you.'

Those were his words, and to this date, those were the words that Jason had followed. He was a simple boy, but he was a simple, independent boy. He didn't need his mother to sing him to sleep at night, he didn't need lights to sleep at night and he for sure didn't need anyone beside him, giving him the support that anyone else would need to live on and to survive, for that is how he had grown up to be strong and powerful.

'Alright, Jason, calm down. No god is going to listen to you if you cry out here like this, no god.' Jason thought as he slowly calmed down and controlled his breathing. He didn't want to be cooped up here like this, and he didn't want to stay here just because he couldn't do something to get out. He needed to get out and return home to his family and friends. He needed to get out of here or nothing was going to happen to him. 'Let's think, think, think. Alright, the guys are going to come behind me if I escape, so I have to be smart about things. I know that there are three males out here, and for me to escape, I need to cut through these rags. Thankfully, the best thing that I can do here is to actually think about these things properly.'

Shaking his head and appearing to be in control over himself, Jason grinned. He knew that they should have cut his overgrown nails, he just knew it. If they had done that, then it wouldn't have come to this, ever. His nails were large enough for him to actually chip off slightly, and sure they hurt, but after some time, he was able to actually make a nice, small cut in the rag. He knew that this wasn't supposed to be happening, but either these kidnappers were really desperate for the money, or they were out of supplies. The only problem was going to be the door, which was locked. And for him to escape out of the door, he would need for them to actually come in first. But if he took one out, then the other two would be behind him as well.

'Alright. First order of business, get to know your

surroundings well,' the boy thought. He had to get out of here and then find a way to know where he was kept. And for that, he just had to wait for the right time. It would be a delicate process but he would have to be really smart about this, and for that to happen, he needed to be silent and sneaky. He praised his luck that he managed to get his hands and legs free by using his chipped off thumbnails and then picked up the rags and tied himself up properly again, this time, in a way that he could actually use his hands and legs.

And he knew that this was the perfect time because it was dinner time.

"Well, kiddo, it seems that luck is with you today. We've got some leftover pizza." The fat, smelly, disgusting oaf of a warden came into the room. He was smelling as bad as the rags and he was looking as disgusting as the status of the room itself. And this was the man that he was going to strike, one way or the other. He wanted the man to just pass out, some-way, somehow. He wanted that to happen and he was going to make that a reality. And right now, he just had to think properly, just think about things and he would succeed. "Alright, where do I begin? Open your mouth."

But Jason stopped before he could begin. He knew that he would need the energy, and as bad as the pizza looked, he would still have to eat it somehow. So, he opened his mouth and let the man feed him the disgusting looking Pizza. And he almost made a face when the cold and obviously rotten taste of meat touched his tongue. He had a plan for this as well. He would stick the rotten pieces of meat to the side of his mouth and only eat the bread and the cheese, and after that was done, he would try to spit them out on a later date. As he ate the Pizza, Jason noticed that the door was left open and that was his chance.

As the last piece went into his mouth, Jason twitched his legs so he could use them. He simply swiped down off to the side of the man and grinned as the large, heavy-set man fell down to the ground in a large cry. He couldn't believe how big of an idiot this man was. Ripping apart the rags that he had purposefully tied so he could get up, he grabbed the plate and slammed it right on the man's head so hard that the man could barely see straight. Another slam was enough to knock him out in a deep sleep. Then he waited. For 10 full seconds, he waited, and since no one came, he just kept the tray with him, a nice, hard, metallic tray, and spat the rotten pieces of meat out on the man. Grinning widely, Jason merrily went on his way, ignoring everything else.

Getting out of the room was easy enough. He knew that there was someone out there waiting for the fat man to come back again, and he wasn't going to take any chances. He had to be smart about things, and strong as well. The only way he was going to succeed was by being smart. And smart he was.

He had to learn, he had to improvise and he had to observe. He could hear some rummaging in the area right beside the main room and the sound of the TV in the main room. So, that meant there were only two other people, he knew it. The first one was in the kitchen and the second one inside the main room.

So, he would go up against the one in the kitchen first, and then the one in the living room. That was the only way that this could work and the only way that this would be normal. The only way that this could go wrong right now would be if he made a mistake, and Jason didn't like mistakes at all. Nope, he did not. So, that is why he became even sneakier than he already was. He became the sneakiest that he could be and was slowly sneaking down to the ground floor of the house that he was in, and directly to the kitchen.

This guy was not fat and slender. But he was short and was definitely not knowing of him. Walking closer to him, he slammed the tray hard on the man's head, and Jason watched as the man came toppling down. He ran towards the edge of the door that led to the main room and waited at the side to see if someone would come in. Luckily, no one did, the voice of the TV was too loud for the third and probably the last person that was to know that something was horribly wrong.

He walked sneakily inside of the living room, looking up at the TV to find out what his location was. The first thing he saw was the slight snow outside in the tropical rainforest-like area. So, he was up north. Then he noticed the slightest difference between the actress and the News Channel that was on. It was a weather forecast. So, that would mean he was in CANADA!

'Alright. I am in Canada, what now?' Jason thought as he walked closer to the back of the couch. Another hard slam later, the third and the final guy was also knocked unconscious. Now was the start of the timer. According to him, he had three hours to get as far away from this place as he could. And that was not considering what else was out there. So, he had to run, and as fast as he could run at that. And he was going to run. But first, some supplies. Luckily, he was right beside the kitchen and there was some fresh food, water, and some weapons that he could use. Sure, it was a slight popper that he didn't have any guns, but he at least had knives, some canned survival food, and a radio of sorts. Even if he could give out a signal to someone, he had to know what was going on. He just had to.

And so, Jason Smith, after 10 full days of captivity in a shack in presumably Canada, got away from his captors.

CHAPTER TWO

Jason ran.

Jason wasn't sure how long he had been running for when the wolves noticed there had been a person, but he could hear them barking to one another when they began to follow him. Jason knew he could never outrun them. (The wolf runs on average 42-60 miles per hour. It's been known to track its prey for days on end. It rarely needs more than a few minutes, though.) He needed to do something, or he would die.

A tree.

His parents always had terrible trouble grounding him. The main problem was due to the tree that was outside his window. Jason hated being trapped inside and took every chance to escape by climbing up and down that tree. He had become incredibly good at climbing because of this. It had gotten so bad that his parents put an alarm on his window that went off whenever he opened it.

The alarm had been magnetic. Jason would always just take a magnet off the kitchen fridge and stick it on the alarm so that the device wouldn't realize the connection had been interrupted. It didn't stop him from sneaking out. His parents never figured it out.

Jason saw a tree large enough about fifteen feet ahead of him. The branches were out of his reach but that wasn't a problem. He kicked off the truck and shot up his hands to grab the lowest branch. Moving quickly, he swung up his legs and started to climb. Just in the nick of time, too. The wolves arrived just as he began to climb, and Jason felt the breeze of their snapping jaws as they tried to bite him and the scurrying of their claws as they tried to get up to the top of the tree.

Jason didn't look down. He didn't stop climbing. He just kept moving until the branches got so thin that they risked snapping. Finally, he stopped. Leaning against the trunk as he caught his breath, he looked down at the ground below.

The wolves were still there.

They were snarling and pacing below the tree, their claws still bloody from the mauling of some poor animal, or human. Then, the largest wolf leaped towards the tree. Its claws dug into the bark and held. It was climbing the tree.

Jason pressed against the tree in fear. He had to tightly cover his mouth with his hands to keep from screaming. He had been wrong. The tree wouldn't save him; it just made it harder for them to get to him. But he had trapped himself in the process. He couldn't climb anymore; the branches would snap if he went up and he'd pass right by the wolf if he went down. He couldn't jump to the ground, it was too high and there were still three wolves at the bottom. He closed his eyes and prayed to any deity that may be listening to save him. A crashing sound answered him.

The wolf was on the ground again, even angrier than it had been before. It was limping slightly on one foot, snarling and barking at its companions. The deep gouges in the tree answered Jason's unspoken question. It had fallen.

The wolves stayed for several more minutes before leaving. Jason waited with bated breath for any sign of them before beginning the trip back down the tree. Carefully, he placed his foot on a branch.

It snapped under his weight, and the branch fell to the ground with a dull thud.

The wolves swarmed out of their hiding place. Scrambling to pull himself back up, Jason beat a hasty retreat up the tree. The wolves had actually waited to see what he would do. They were so much smarter than he had thought. Than anyone had thought. And that scared him more than anything else that had happened that day.

It rained that night.

Tropical storms tended to come out of nowhere and leave just as quickly as they came. But while they were there, they were fierce, howling things that battered you with rain and wind until all you could do was cling, shivering to yourself as you waited for it to pass. It was in that manner that Jason spent the night.

The only good outcome of the storm was that it drove the wolves away. He had seen them disappear into the trees, illuminated by flashes of lightning.

'They must be returning to their den', Jason thought. 'Or they could just be sitting aside to see what I would do.' chimed in his pessimistic side. Before leaving the tree, he broke off branches and threw them to the ground in hopes of causing any waiting wolves to reveal themselves. None came, but Jason feared that was because they had learned to wait before pouncing.

Still, he couldn't spend the rest of his (quite possibly very short) life in a tree. Cautiously, he moved down the branches and hopped the remaining distance to the ground.

A bush rattled. His heart stopped. A small snake slithered out of the foliage and Jason sighed in relief. While turning to leave the area, he saw it. A large sickle claw was lodged into the bark of the tree. The wolf had been limping, Jason remembered. At the time, he had thought it was due to the fall, but apparently, it had lost a claw in the process, causing the limp. The claw still had some blood on it.

With an amazingly steady hand, Jason reached up and yanked it out of the wood. He stumbled backward with the force of it, but he had achieved his goal. The claw was now resting in the palm of his hand, just as wicked sharp and deadly as it had been the day before.

Wiping it on his pant leg, Jason realized that the claw could be incredibly useful to him. It could be used as a weapon while he was on the run to safety. It could be used to cut, to kill and even to get him some much-needed food. He could have used it to cut him free of the sail. They would have been gone before the wolves ever found them. This claw could help him survive.

Survive.

Jason knew that would be difficult. Canada had been declared the most difficult place to survive on the planet in the wild. But he also knew he would fight until his last breath. He wasn't exactly a slouch when it came to the wilderness. Jason had always loved camping (just not with wild animals that would tear him apart and kill him) and was an avid Boy Scout. Between what he knew about the wild and that, he could survive until the rescue teams came.

And that had to be soon, right? Right? The world would know that someone was missing, his parents would report it to the police and the police would report it to the army and all of that, and help was going to come finally, right?

Help wasn't coming.

It took Jason three days to figure that out. Three days of watching the skies, listening for planes, and praying that someone, anyone would come for him. Three days of nothing. He had been sitting around in the same area that he was when he hid from the wolves, and he knew for certain that help wasn't coming.

If they were coming for him, they'd have been here long ago. In this part of the country, things tend to die quickly. People die quickly. They wouldn't have dragged their feet when it was a twelve-year-old. No, the only thing they expected to find of him were the parts the animals hadn't liked. And they weren't going to risk more lives to find pieces of a body. They had already decided he had died in this place. And because of that, he would die in this country.

It may not be that day. It may not be the next. But he

would die there eventually, and it would probably be soon.

He knew that he should keep up hope for a rescue, but it was hard to be hopeful when you were at the bottom of the food chain. Frustrated, Jason kicked the trunk of a tree. It wasn't fair. He hadn't deserved to land on this godforsaken place. He didn't deserve to be here. He was Jason Smith! He was supposed to be at home in his nice warm bed.

Jason wanted to scream. He wanted to cry. So, he did. He cried for everything he had lost because of those kidnappers and for himself. He picked up a stick and beat it against the nearest tree and let out all the frustration and fear that had been churning inside him ever since he had escaped from the Kidnappers, then sank to the ground as he continued to cry.

All it did was attract the Lizards.

One of the Lizards that he knew, not the scientific name but the local name from a Biology class, was the Red-Golden Lizard. It was one of the very few Lizards that would hunt in packs and was very, very, very savvy with the wild and avoiding larger prey and animals. It was very smart and it knew what to do and what not to do. Alone, the Red-Golden Lizard wasn't anything to fear as it was very small.

But as a pack, it was known to attack, kill and eat larger organisms. And if you were lucky, it was in that order.

The Redgs (a short name for them) were poisonous. There was a neurotoxin in its saliva that made its victim feel befuddled, drowsy, and altogether content. They didn't even mind when the Redgs began to eat them alive.

The chirping was what first alerted Jason to their presence. The first one hopped into view, looking at him curiously with its reddish-golden skin and deep black eyes. It was the scout. The one that determined whether they would be able to successfully attack their prey.

And in this case, it decided they would attack Jason.

It made an odd chirping noise, and suddenly, there wasn't just one Redg. There was at least a dozen, all surrounding him. Jason quickly shot back to his feet and glanced around. There wasn't anything he could use for a weapon in arms reach.

Sharp pain in his arm drew his attention back to the Lizards. One had leaped onto him and had dug its teeth into his wrist. Quickly, he tore it off, but it was too late. Jason could already feel the ice-cold venom slowly making its way down his arm. He kicked a path in the Redgs and began to run. The sixteen-year-old could hear the strange chirps and hisses as they followed. He ran faster.

Then, he climbed another tree. Jason had a feeling that he'd be getting very familiar with trees soon if he lived that long. He could hear them still hissing and chirping at the base of the tree, but he had the feeling they'd move on soon. They probably had a much shorter attention span than Wolves. For now, he had bigger problems.

The poison.

He wasn't sure if it was fatal or not. The popular consensus had been that it was temporary, only slowing their victims rather than outright killing them. However, no one really knew since the Redgs tended to eat their victims before anyone could find out. And there was no living human specimen of the Lizards as most tended to avoid facing them, or simply killed them all as fast as they could. Besides, there was no way a little Lizard like that would try and eat him, right?

Either way, Jason didn't want it in his body. He yanked off his belt and wrapped it tightly around his upper arm. It would function as a temporary tourniquet. Then, he brought his lips to the wound. They had taught him this in Scouts, but then it had been used for snakebites. This was (just a tad) different. Carefully, Jason began to suck the venom from the bite and immediately spat it out. Then, he repeated the process. He continued until his arm had gone numb from the tourniquet and there was a sour taste in his mouth. He leaned back against the tree and began to fumble with the belt. Finally managing to loosen it, he pulled it off and sighed in exhaustion.

That couldn't happen again. Jason knew that there was every likelihood that he'd be attacked by some other creature, but he couldn't let it happen again due to that reason.

The Redgs were attracted to sick and injured animals, and Jason knew his cries had certainly made him sound like the easy, pre-maimed that the Lizards and other scavengers enjoyed. He had almost been eaten alive because of his outburst back there.

'No more crying' he decided. 'No matter how bad it gets, crying won't help. It'll only make it worse. That is what Grandfather said, remember.'

Jason glanced back down the tree again. The Lizards were gone. He doubted they'd be able to be like the Wolves, actually waiting for him to come back down. Slowly, he began his trek back down the tree. He jumped the remaining distance to the ground and stumbled as he landed. The venom was still making him dizzy, even if it was mostly gone. Steadying himself, he began to move through the woods.

Jason had found a building.

It wasn't a particularly impressive building, but it was a building nonetheless, and it managed to foster hope in Jason that maybe there was a way to call for help.

He should have known better than to hope.

While there were phones, none of them actually worked. There wasn't even any power in the building, nothing electrical in the compound worked. It was supposed to be a Military bunker and when they had abandoned it, they hadn't left any weapons behind; there wasn't anything he could use to defend himself against the Country's other 'residents.'

But that didn't mean he hadn't found anything helpful. The building was a gold mine of information. Apparently, this bunker was supposed to be a bomb testing site and not a normal bomb, but some sort of frag grenade and other C4-like bombs. It wasn't anything Nuclear in nature, but he wouldn't be surprised if there was something that wasn't supposed to be here. He also found the exact coordinates of the building, and the Radio that he had gotten from his captors could be used to get a message to someone out there. What's more, they had left behind supplies. Jason could salvage food, lanterns, and medicine from the building.

He was tempted to stay in the compound, but he knew he couldn't. Within a few minutes of entering the building, he could see signs of Wolves, footsteps, other types of things like claw-marks and their ways of marking their territory. While the building wasn't being used as a den, it was still frequented by the animals. It wasn't a safe place to stay.

Still, Jason couldn't bring himself to leave the first sign of humanity he'd seen since escaping from the Kidnappers. He stayed there that night, curled up in an old desk chair in an attempt to sleep. And he always did wonder if the Nabbers tried to find out where he had gone. It had almost been five days since he had escaped. Surely, they would have tried something.

———

When Jason was younger, his mother had taken him to a cathedral.

Religion had been another thing his parents had fought about. His father operated an exacting, precise logic. He hadn't believed in something as intangible as God. His mother, however, was driven by wild thoughts and fervent emotion. You don't have to see something to believe in it, she had whispered to him. The best things are the ones taken on faith. Faith had been important to her, Jason remembered. It had driven her to continue to return to church every Sunday, no matter how many fights it caused.

Then, one day, she had taken Jason with her.

Jason hadn't been sure about God. He had been torn between his parents, unsure about their opposing viewpoints. However, he had come with her that day. And he never forgot that church.

His footsteps had echoed on the floor, the sound bouncing off the walls and multiplying in the air. He had looked up at the glass windows above him and watched as the dust danced through the light and he felt... something. Jason wasn't sure if it was God. If it was faith. But he had felt it weigh on him, the solemn air of something more.

And as Jason walked through the abandoned missile control room, he was reminded of that feeling.

It wasn't the sacred aura that the cathedral had held. It was very, very different. This room held the remains of crossed lines and shattered dreams. It was advanced that really didn't advance at all, just monstrous ideas come to life. Jason felt like something was trying to crawl up his skin and take root, to forever become a part of his mind and soul.

This room was weighed down with a thousand ghosts.

Jason shook his head. The wild was already making him paranoid. While the room was spooky, there was nothing supernatural about it. No ghost was going to come screaming towards him. No monster would leap at him as he turned the corner like in Cheesy B films.

Then, Jason heard the soft sounds of footsteps behind him, and he re-evaluated his opinion. Normally, he wouldn't have been able to hear anything. The steps were soft, just the barely notice-able pad of bare feet on a solid surface. If it weren't for the impressive resonating acoustics (oh, so like that church so long ago) in the room, Jason would have never been able to hear it. Quickly, he hid behind an overturned table and waited.

It was a wolf. The animal didn't seem to be aware of his presence, not yet at least. It was making leisurely, calm sweeps with its head as it lazily inspected the room. 'What is it doing?' Jason wondered.

Suddenly, the wolf paused and began to sniff the air. Jason's breath caught in his throat. In all likelihood, the thing it was smelling was him. He had to get out of the building. The only problem with that plan was the fact that the wolf was between him and the exit.

If he made a run for it, he would be seen and, most likely, killed. The wolf, still sniffing curiously, began to slowly pad its way towards Jason's hiding place. He inched his way backward, only to hit a wall. He couldn't retreat from his position without being seen.

Jason's hand brushed against his pocket. Maybe he could.

While he was exploring the compound, he had discovered smoke grenades. They hadn't seemed particularly useful at the time. They didn't even produce tear gas, just a harmless cloud of vapor. But, they could be used to hide his retreat now. If they worked, that is. He hadn't been able to test them, so there was every chance that they wouldn't work. And if they failed, the wolf would know where he was and he would have nothing to defend himself with.

Jason took in a shaky breath and came to a decision. He'd still be found if he didn't use the grenade. His best chance would be to try it and hope for the best. With unsteady hands, he took the device from his pocket and pulled the pin. Then, he rolled it away from the hiding place and towards the animal. It teetered to a stop right next to the wolf. Jason held his breath as the carnivore bent down to sniff it.

Nothing was happening!

He closed his eyes in defeat. He was dead. Then, an unusual barking sound grabbed his attention. His eyes flew open. The wolf was making a strange, pained choking sound. Smoke was pouring out of the grenade, clouding the air. A smile planted itself on his face as the wolf stumbled backward. It was working. Not wasting time, he sprinted through the cloud and out of the room, skidding into the wall as he turned the corner. He heard the cawing of the wolf as it began to pursue. Jason could see the exit. It was fifty feet away. Forty. Twenty-five. Fifteen. Then, Jason saw it. There was a metal gate that rolled down from the ceiling, like the kind that his dad used in his plumbing supplies store in the mall, at the intersection before the doors. Not breaking stride, Jason tensed his legs and jumped. His hands grabbed the bottom of the grate, and for a horrible moment, he feared it wouldn't move. But then it gave with a screech and came rumbling down towards the ground. Jason tumbled to a stop against the door as it slammed into the ground. Then, an enormous crash brought his eyes shooting towards the partition.

The wolf had slammed into it seconds after it locked into place. Frustrated, it slammed its body into the gate again and again. The metal creaked and bent, but remained locked in place. A small smile touched the corners of Jason's mouth, but vanished the moment the wolf let loose a deep, guttural howling noise.

It was calling for help.

Jason didn't want to be there when help arrived. He pulled himself to his feet and threw open the double doors. Then, he fled into the long grasses, praying that wherever he ended up would be safer than where he left.

Jason found his luck was a mixed bag.

On one hand, he seemed to have found shelter. On the other hand, he may have given himself a concussion in the process.

After fleeing the military compound, he had stumbled into the treeline. He didn't stop, though; he needed to put as much distance between himself and the wolves as possible. He did learn, however, through (quite a painful) experience that he should have slowed down, if only slightly. He had been darting through the branches as quickly as he could when the ground gave out from under him. He tumbled down the newly discovered hill and quite literally clanged to a stop.

Rubbing his head, Jason looked up to see what he slammed into. In front of him was a large water truck that had been trapped in a gorge. Yanking himself to his feet, he began to slowly inspect the vehicle. There was a steel door on the side of the overturned truck. Jason winced as it creaked open. Anything could have heard that. Carefully, he pulled himself through the opening and dropped to the floor within. He glanced around the dreary space. It was dark, damp, and cold. The steel of the walls felt like ice against his skin and there were still puddles of water inside the container. But, there were large metal bolts that could be drawn against the trap door. It could be used to keep animals and insects out.

Jason smiled to himself. This could work. He didn't care what poor sod ended up in such an accident, or how old this water truck was because it did seem like a very old model. This meant two things. There used to be a motorway here and he knew that the ground was strange around the area, he just hadn't noticed it properly. And if there was once a Motorway there years ago, then another one, however unused it was, wouldn't be far. This water truck was a remain along with the Military compound, and it was going to be his hiding place, at least until he got an idea as to where he was and what he was doing. After that, though, this was the only way he was going to be able to escape.

The last place Jason wanted to go was back towards the Wolves, but he had no choice. He needed the supplies in the building. Besides, the wolves had probably moved on long ago.

Or at least that was what Jason kept telling himself.

Cautiously, Jason pulled himself out of his new, temporary home and glanced around. There didn't appear to be any animals, insects, Redgs or anyone in sight. He glanced up at the sky. In Scouts, they had learned to tell the time by looking at the sun. Based on Jason's estimation, there was still a good four or five hours of sunlight left. He would need them. Slowly, he set out towards the Military Missile complex. While the trip took quite a bit more time, he avoided cracking his head against the side of a giant metal car again.

He reached the building with no trouble. Carefully, he inched open the doors and glanced inside. There wasn't a wolf in sight; not that meant much. He crept inside and looked around. Immediately, he was thankful he hadn't stuck around earlier. The reinforced steel gate that Jason had used to block the wolf hadn't held up against whatever assistance the creature had called for. All that was left of it was a warped bunch of chains hanging from the ceiling. He began to make his way through the compound, intently listening for any signs of Wolves.

He made his way to the supply room without a confrontation. The Military had kept their facilities well stocked, and they hadn't had any time to clear out before abandoning it. If he carefully rationed it, he'd have enough for years.

If he lived that long, that is.

Jason slowly began to move supplies over to his water truck. He wasn't going to bring everything; that would take too long and take up too much space. Instead, he just brought enough food and lanterns (actually, why did they even have those and how old was this base for them to use bulb lanterns that worked on batteries and not LED flashlights that could last three times as long?) for a few weeks. That way, if something happened that limited his ability to move about the area, he'd be able to hunker down in his truck for at least a couple weeks before coming back. It took a while to move the supplies as he had to make multiple trips, but it was worth it.

Jason tugged a lab coat off its hanger. The water truck was cold, and while the jacket was thin, it would provide at least a little warmth. He swung it on and frowned curiously at the weight inside its pocket. A small, leather journal was resting inside the coat; it must have been forgotten when the Military Base Scientist or doctor had left the base. Jason glanced through it inquisitively. Whoever it belonged to must have just started it as there were only a few pages used, and all of it was in a strange foreign, coded language that the Military had employed. He couldn't understand a word. Shrugging, he slipped it back in his pocket.

Jason glanced around the center. He had already moved all the food he would need and take all the smoke grenades in case he ran into any Wolves. He wouldn't have time for any more trips; he didn't want to be out after dark. He slung the First Aid kit he had found over his shoulder and got ready to leave when something caught his eye. The center had a line of well-stocked vending machines rusting in the corner. While it would be comforting to have a bit of traditional, rot your teeth candy, the power was out. He couldn't exactly shove in a quarter and get a chocolate bar. He glanced around for something to break the Plexiglass with. While he had been studying Brazilian Jiu-Jitsu since he was a little kid (his security-minded, be-prepared-for-any-eventuality father had insisted on Jason learning self-defense. He hadn't minded as he actually enjoyed the lessons), he didn't trust himself to be able to break the glass with his foot, not without injuring himself. Then, he remembered something. Quickly, he headed back to the other room and rifled through a desk drawer. He snagged a screwdriver from the opening along with a broken bit of a metal bar that had been discarded on the ground and hurried back. There, he rested the head of the screwdriver against the Plexiglass and brought the metal bar down on top of it. A complex pattern of cracks spider-webbed across the surface of the machine. Jason repeated the process and his makeshift tools crashed through the opening. He smirked at the victory and dug out a few of the bars. These would have to be even more strictly rationed than the food.

Carefully, he set back out for his new home, inspecting his surroundings as he went. Jason would have to be on high alert as he traversed the wilderness. With a sinking feeling, he realized he would likely have to be on high alert for the rest of his life unless he found a way to get the hell out of this place.

Jason plopped against the floor of the truck with a sigh. By all accounts, it had been a good day. He had only been attacked by animals once, and he managed to escape without a scratch. He had found supplies and had gained valuable knowledge about how to survive.

'If those are my standards for a good day, something must be seriously wrong with me.' He thought.

Still, he missed his mom and dad, they had been good parents. They never stopped loving Jason, even if they stopped loving each other at times. His eyes burned at the thought of them. He would give anything to see them one more time.

'They probably think I'm dead.' He thought. 'Just like everyone else.'

Jason took a deep breath and forced himself not to

cry. He had only promised himself yesterday that he would stop crying; he wasn't about to break that promise. He just wished there was a way to let people know that he wasn't dead yet. Even if it wasn't found for thirty years and he had been killed long before, he wanted them to know that he hadn't died so easily. That he had survived, if only for a little while. With a groan, he turned on his side and tried to sleep.

There was a bulge in his pocket.

Jason remembered the journal he had found earlier and knew that if he didn't manage to escape, someone would have to know where he was and find this place no matter how many years it would take. He knew that he would try his best to get the hell out of whatever part of Canada he was in, but he didn't know how long that would take and it would probably kill him in the end. But he did have a journal. And, one day, it may be found. He sat up, sleep instantly forgotten. This notebook could be a chance, he realized. A chance to say goodbye to his parents, a chance to let them know exactly how long he lasted here. He could let them know that he loved them, even if he wasn't there to say it in person.

Jason yanked the leather-bound book out of his pocket and flipped it open. Scrambling in his pockets for a pen, he pulled that out as well. The low glow of the lantern cast strange shadows on the paper, but Jason didn't mind. Then, he paused. What would he write? What could he possibly say about the situation he was in?

He could hear the noises of the wild outside of his metal walls. The roars of the predators, the howling of the wind, the screeches of pain and fear from the newly prey. This was the closest anyone would ever know about what it was like in prehistoric times, Jason realized, the only way he would understand the life of their ancestors, always fearing for the worst. At least he wasn't actually in those times. He didn't know what he would do if he was actually in such places. Jason guiltily wished that the honor belonged to anyone but him. His resolve strengthened, he lowered the pen to paper and began to write.

I guess I should start with the fact that my name is Jason Smith, I'm sixteen years old, and I'm not dead. Yet.

That night the wind howled, the prey screamed, and the predators roared. But Jason barely noticed.

He was too busy writing. And after he was done writing, he remembered. He had a Radio and the co-ordinates of the buildings.

He thought about it. He knew that he couldn't stay close to the building. Relying on only one thing to get someone out of a problem was a very bad idea, Jason knew that. And that wasn't what he wanted to do. Jason knew that if he was going to be smart about things and be thinking about things, then the only way that he would survive the wild would be if he moved about. If he actually used his brains and moved around the area, and tried to find a way to escape, tried to find a way to live and tried to find a way to get out of the wild. And for that to happen, he would have to leave this place, this water truck, and the compound. But he could at least send a message in.

Remembering everything he could about the various survival tricks he had learned in the Boy Scouts and the shows he had seen on TV, Jason slowly activated the Radio. Upon the first sound of the loud static, he closed it and waited with bated breath, hoping that no one heard it. Luckily, no one had. Nothing was heard and no one had come. So, Jason knew that he would have to muffle the sound. Luckily, he had enough rags to do that, and carefully setting the frequency that was on the piece of paper with the co-ordinates, Jason tried his luck again.

"To any stations, this is Jason Smith. Can anyone hear me?" His reply was cold, hard silence. He knew that this was stupid and that a Military radio station wouldn't work. "I repeat, to any stations, this is Jason Smith, can anyone hear me?"

There was, once again, no reply, and Jason's will dropped. But he remembered. He knew that the military didn't need to acknowledge anything. So, he started talking.

"I am a sixteen-year-old boy that has escaped from his kidnappers by managing to knock them out using a tray. I don't know if this message goes through or not, but I am in the wilderness of Canada around the location with the coordinates--" Jason read out the coordinates. "It belonged to an abandoned military bunker and I am around a twenty-minute walk to the south of the Bunker inside of a water truck. I hope this message travels across. I am a boy from 8,

Chester Street, Southern Boulevard, New York, United States of America. Jason. You can contact my parents, Tyler Smith and Melissa Smith if you wish. I have been missing for approximately twenty-five days. Please, send help. I will be here for five days more and then I will leave. I repeat, please send help."

And then all that was heard inside of the water truck was the cold, hard darkness.

CHAPTER THREE

Jason pushed as close to the end of the branch as he dared. As he predicted, he had become extremely accustomed to trees in his time in the Wilderness. However, it was not due to the reasons he imagined. He still used it as a means to escape carnivores, but recently, he had begun to use them for very different functions.

Like now.

Jason had discovered a valley. It was enclosed by steep sides that funneled into narrow openings at both ends. A long river snaked through the area, and on top of the walls of the valley, there were tall trees that branched over the edge.

That was where Jason was now.

The valley was a thriving ecosystem frequented by herbivores. Bulls marched by the river, bison roamed in herds, and the rare foxes and badgers stampeded through the grass. A part of him wished he could enter the valley itself, even if he knew he would likely get trampled. And that wasn't even the main danger.

The biggest danger was the Wolves.

There were at least three packs of wolves in the fields, Jason had discovered. The first pack nested in an old abandoned maintenance building on the other end of the country. Jason, rightly valuing his life, had never entered the complex. Jason wasn't entirely certain where the second nest was located, but, based on the territory that the pack patrolled, he suspected it was near where he had first encountered the Wolves. That was likely the reason for whatever animals the wolf had killed before coming to get him; he had gotten too close to the den. And the third pack was located on the edges of this valley.

Jason jerked his head towards the sound of the bison

howling and huffing and snarling and doing whatever sound they could while they bathed in the water. Immediately, he brought a pair of pilfered binoculars to his eyes and began scanning the field. He had a theory about this behavior and he wanted to see it confirmed.

He smiled in triumph as he saw the bison herd automatically turn their bodies around, swinging their long, defensive horns in a protective arc. The fox clustered closer behind the larger animals, and Jason knew he had been right.

When he had first stumbled on this valley, one of the first things he had noticed was the unusual behaviorisms of the bison and the foxes. They always remained clustered together, regardless of the cross-species differences. Then, he developed a hypothesis.

Jason had learned about it in biology class. In Africa, zebras, with their good sense of smell, and baboons, with their fantastic eyesight, often remained close together because they were more effective against predators as a team. This mutually beneficial relationship had been called inter-species symbiosis.

And bison, who possessed incredibly strong defensive horns yet terrible eyesight, would greatly benefit from the weak but clear-sighted foxes. A mutual predator defense, even if one of them said animals was a predator, and the Fox could betray the bison anytime he wanted. But the bison herd was larger than the Fox herd. And even if he had only spent eight days in the water truck, three days longer in the hopes that someone would come for him, he still needed to find out more about these animals.

Now, he just had to locate the predator.

Jason watched as the streaks of greenish-brown darted across the field. Automatically, many of the herds clustered into a defensive form around their children. Jason spotted the aptly named "good mother" of the bison with the babies standing around her, but that wouldn't save them from the wolves. The Gray wolf was a pack hunter and in this deadly cold, things weren't all that easy.

Jason couldn't help but be a little... awestruck at their attack strategies. The killing machines darted in and out of gaps, separating the herd and striking at the weakest links. They quickly dragged away from their kill, snapping at anything that approached. The bison herd thundered and cried, with the one that Jason suspected to be the prey's mother being the loudest, but it was too late. There was nothing they could do to save their children.

They couldn't even leave the valley.

What astonished Jason the most was the fact that the wolves were herding the animals. They had corralled them into space and attacked anything that tried to leave. While the wolves wisely did not hinder the coming and going of some of the predators, like the Grizzly bears that frequented the area, anything small enough to bring down was trapped inside, destined to be struck down at the leisure of the predators.

It was intelligent. It was sophisticated. And it was not what scientists speculated about wolves at all. For them, the wolves were nothing but insane, abandoning, heartless creatures, but it was now that Jason found out, that wasn't the case.

Ironically enough, one of the earliest theories about wolves was closest to reality. They never abandoned their pack mates unless they did the worse of their crimes, or one turned out to be a lone wolf.

They would always stay behind for their pack mates and any time one of their pack died, their howls would be deep and loud. And as if mourning with them, the other packs would also howl, loudly at that.

Jason pulled out his journal and hastened to record the behaviors of the animals. Like the trees, his original function for the notebook had changed. At first, it was a way to maybe let his parents know what had happened to him. Now, however, it was part field journal, part how-to-survive-in-this-crazy-country cheat sheet for any future castaways. He did leave a note in the journal for whoever found it, asking that they gave it to his parents if and when they managed to escape.

And that was a big "if."

Jason had tried, of course, to find a way off. He had lugged palm branches up to the roof of the lab and built an 'SOS' message for any passing planes. The problem was, no planes passed over this particular area. It was very rarely used, and no one was actually stupid enough to fly over it for the fear of the distance it had from the nearest airport.

Which meant there were zero results from that attempt at rescue.

Then, Jason had tried to make his way to the borders. He knew that he wasn't all that deep in the country, he just knew it. From using one of the maps inside of the Military bunker and the other store-room on the other side of the entire damned area that he was trapped in, he knew the location of the water truck, and he was only around 100 miles away from the borders, a distance he could travel in one and a half months. But there was one problem. The wolves were very, very smart and didn't allow anyone to leave their 'circle' of influence and their territories.

All of his escape attempts had the exact same results: failure.

Suddenly, the branch he was on shook under him. Jason's eyes shot up, looking for the disturbance, and his breath caught in his throat at the sight that greeted him.

A bear. It was perched on its hind legs to reach the trees, calmly biting off huge mouthfuls of whatever it was eating. Grizzly bears were omnivores, he realized, and they wouldn't only eat meat but could survive off of fruits and berries as well. Jason watched as it fell back to all fours, shaking the ground as it landed due to its immense size, at least compared to him. Then, it bent its maw towards the ground. Curious, Jason leaned over to see what it was doing. A much younger bear, a baby really, was following closely behind its bigger counterpart. The parent was feeding its child, offering it some of the berries still hanging out of its mouth. Jason smiled as it tumbled over itself to get to the food, its little neck unbalancing the still-growing animal. Then, the adult raised back on its hind legs and returned to the tree.

And it looked at Jason.

Slowly, Jason lifted his hand, not breaking its massive gaze. Then, he carefully pressed his hand against the furry animal.

The brachiosaur didn't move away from Jason's caress. It just stared at him with large, intelligent orbs, as if it knew who he was. Bears were supposed to be wild and extremely harsh. But this one was docile. It could sense that he wasn't going to harm and was only observing, so it didn't attack.

Hot puffs of the animal's breath blew on his face, rustling his hair. Shakily, Jason smiled.

Then, the bear pulled back, falling down to the ground, shaking the ground as it landed. It nudged its child with its head and turned around, the two creatures heading off towards the slowly descending sun.

Jason watched them leave. He clenched the fist that had touched the bear. There were no words for what he had just experienced. But he did know one thing...

He didn't hate this Country. He didn't even hate wildlife.

If he had the choice, he'd leave in an instant. He'd go home to his mom and dad and try to move past everything that had happened here. He'd try to forget all the pain and the horror and the suffering he had experienced. But he would never hate the animals. People tended to only see this country as one thing. Some saw it as a fantastic paradise, a world away from their hectic lives in Canada. They only had awestruck images of kindly, parental humans that would allow humans to intrude and meddle with their lives. They saw unintelligent, benevolent creatures that could be poked and prodded without consequence. They saw the illusion the TV had tried to create, and they only saw the human settlements, but not the wilderness. They would never get to see the wilderness. On a level, they knew that the wildlife was dangerous, but they didn't truly understand what that meant. In their minds, humans would always be on the top of the food chain, and no other predator could change that.

Others, like some of the Politicians, only saw this country as a waste of time and money at times, as if it was meant for them to make fun of, but they were wrong. They were all wrong, every single one of them.

This country had more than one side to it. It had predators that stalked and parents that doted and herds that roamed. It was a thousand different things, all mixing together and interacting and alive. This country had animals on it that were complex and intelligent and, yes, dangerous, but undeniably more so if you disrespected them as so many others had.

And Jason didn't hate them for being dangerous. It was just their nature. There was no malevolent intent, just deep-rooted primal instinct that dictated how they lived and survived.

Jason didn't even hate the Wolves. In fact, now he even loved them.

They had killed various innocent animals. Torn them to shreds right in front of Jason. But they hadn't done it out of some kind of sociopathic urge. They killed them because they were either a threat to the nest, an intruder on their territory, or food. It wasn't for murderous sport for some sick and twisted idea of fun.

Only people killed for those reasons.

Jason glanced at the sun and sighed. While there were still hours of sunlight yet, he needed to head back. He always gave himself hours to return to his water truck, so that if there were any complications on the return trip, he'd still get back before nightfall. If there was one thing Jason was absolutely terrified to experience, it was this wild after dark.

Jason assessed the jump in front of him. He had

made it before, but that didn't necessarily mean that he could make it again.

The problem was the tree. The tree with the best view of the valley didn't have any branches that were low enough to climb. So, he had climbed the neighboring tree and grabbed onto the closest branch. He had to leap to get to it, but he managed it. Now, however, he had to figure out how to do it a second time. Jason took a deep breath and tensed his legs. Then, before he could change his mind, he jumped. His middle smacked into the tree, knocking the breath out of him. He threw his arms around the tree but was already slipping. At last the second, his hands found purchase. Slowly, he pulled himself up, wincing as he went.

Soon, Jason was back on solid ground. He adjusted his leaf covering and carefully set off through the jungle. He had gotten better at traversing the wild, but that didn't mean it was safe. On the contrary, each time he set out, he encountered new and terrifying obstacles like the mad bears, the coyotes, the Wolverines and some of the feral Bobcats. But he had escaped all of them. Only the wolves gave him some form of a challenge and only the wolves would make him truly look at them as if he was a piece of meat for them.

Slowly, Jason had been mapping the area. Originally, he was planning on staying near the bunker, figuring that was where a rescue party would start if they ever came. But then he realized that after two weeks, he shouldn't stay and find his own ways. That was a week ago. He had left the Bunker with all of his supplies and was running towards the border, the only way that he would live. He knew that if he didn't run and if he didn't get out of the area, then there was a chance that he wouldn't ever be free, that he would still be stuck in that horrendous water truck waiting for a rescue that never came. So, he left.

Somehow avoiding the wolf (oh, who was he kidding? He knew that there was another pack right around the corner), he had traveled around 30 miles away from the bunker, using the maps and the compass that he had found, southwards. Crossing rivers using a blow-up raft that he had found in an unused campsite, literally the only thing that it had, he was moving to the borders and he would have to get there as soon as he could.

He wasn't as familiar with this area, however, and he never would be because he had to continue moving. Jason had to move on ahead and leave behind the area he was in, in the fear of being smelt and being caught, but he didn't want to slow down, not one bit. He knew that if he stayed around, then he would be in deeper trouble. And right now, he was in perhaps the last obstacle before he reached the great flat-land he had seen from that mountain. Sure, climbing up and down the large piece of misplaced rock had been an utter pain, but he needed to do it, and he knew that he could see the light of the borders in the distance. There was a base nearby, and that is where he had to go.

And that is where he would go. Getting down from the mountain and towards the plains in the distance, he knew that he was on the right track. Even if no one had received the message, he knew where he was going and what he had to do. Right now, this was his home and this was where he was going to be. And until he got back to New York, there was nothing else that he could do about it. Nothing. So, he just followed the route, and perhaps his earlier calcula-tions had been wrong because he was sure with the lights that he saw that the base was much closer than anticipated.

What really, really made him nervous was the forest that was in front of the base, the forest that he knew he would have to go through at night. That was the only way he would be able to get to the base, as he had taken a rest in an indentation near the mountain for the entire day, and he wasn't about to waste time slacking around. He had to move and perhaps, in the night, he would be able to move faster.

The only problem was the predators that were on the hunt out here at this time of the night. He didn't want to encounter them, not at all. But he was going to have to risk it because it was the only way he'd escape. And that is how he ended up in that situation in the first place. But looking back at it, he would never regret making that decision, because that was what had saved him.

Jason was in trouble. Very, very big trouble.

It had started with the forest. He stayed too late and, instead of moving, he decided to stay around and search the tracks of some of the other wild animals in the area, and that is how he ended up in such a situation. First, it was the Beavers that he never could find close enough, and how they moved around and possibly made dams.

Then, it was the Skunks. The Skunks were also very, very dangerous and they never moved around in packs as their gases would harm even them if they...... farted against someone.

There also just so happened to have been several dozen of them blocking his path.

Jason had been forced to wait while they moved out of the way. He would have gone around, but one direction took him on a one-way scenic trip directly off the edge of a cliff while the other brought him into known wolf territory. He had seen the tracks and the way they had marked the trees. Instead of those interesting routes, he had decided to wait until the Skunks moved on.

And by the time that began to happen, the night was already at its highest and the most dangerous. Which was why Jason was slinking his way through the darkness, clutching his wolf claw and praying he'd make it back alive.

Contrary to popular belief, the fact that it was a jungle did not mean there were a plethora of trees perfect for climbing. Quite unfortunately, many of the trees were unsuited to escape carnivores. Some did not have branches within reach, others had branches that were too weak to support his weight, while others were too short to avoid the jump of the predators. Jason was hoping he'd be able to find one to spend the night in soon, but he didn't think it was likely that he'd have the chance to even make it up a tree.

Because Jason was being hunted.

He could feel their eyes on him, their hungry gazes boring into his skin. He didn't think it was the wolves; they didn't make any sound while they hunted. These were calling back and forth, closing in surely and steadily.

And Jason had no idea what they were. He clutched his claw tighter and stumbled to a stop. He was surrounded. Days in the wild told him this, he was surrounded.

Even if he couldn't hear them, he'd still be able to tell they were there. Jason could see them. The animals' eyes were glowing in the darkness, like a cat. And slowly, those glowing eyes were inching their way towards him.

Pure, blind, primordial fear clutched Jason's heart. They were the predators. He was the prey. And he had no way of changing that fact. They were Coyotes, dangerous pack hunters that wouldn't even wait to tear him apart, especially since they were hungry, very hungry.

Jason was beginning to distinguish some of the features of the Coyotes in the darkness. They weren't all that big; maybe three or four feet tall. Most of that height was taken up by their legs. On the tip of their feet, they had hard claws that were similar to the wolves. Their jaws were filled with small, sharp teeth and their large, bulbous eyes took up most of their heads.

Jason had an idea. A somewhat stupid, Hail-Mary-play of an idea. The Coyotes were nocturnal hunters; they had adapted to accommodate this fact by developing massive eyes that are incredibly sensitive to dim light. It helped them to hunt under the dark canopy of the jungle. It also meant they would be incredibly sensitive to bright light. Perhaps sensitive enough to forget all about the easy meal they were in the process of capturing.

Or, at least Jason hoped they were. He had a few flares in his bag; he had gotten the idea from a book he had read long ago. He thought it may provide a distraction for a wolf if he ever ran into one. Now, however, it looked as if it would provide him with a different service. Slowly, Jason began to creep his left hand into his bag. If he moved too quickly, the coyotes would leap; he had to time this right. His palm passed over several of the objects, searching for the right shape.

The eyes got closer. His hand passed over the fluttering pages of his notebook and the small glass vial of wolf pee he kept for emergencies, don't ask where he got it from, but he kept it with him. He grasped the plastic, cylindrical shape of the flare-

Oh, God.

White-hot pain lanced through Jason's side. With a small, strangled shout, Jason raised his right hand, still gripping the wolf claw, and brought it down on the Coyote's head. The makeshift dagger cleaved into its waxy eye, causing it to release its jaws from the clamp-like grip they had on Jason's side with a shrill howl. The animal stumbled away, still shrieking unnaturally.

The sight provided no comfort to Jason. It was too late; the damage was already done.

He fell to the ground with a dull thud. Jason's hand numbly found his side, coming away slick with hot blood. He could feel the neurotoxin or whatever the saliva of the animal contained begin to work its way into his bloodstream. He knew what was going to happen next. The Coyotes would retreat and wait for the poison to wear him down to the point of no resistance. All of Jason's defenses would slowly be battered down by the neurotoxin, causing hallucinations, then seizures, then paralysis, and finally brain death. He didn't even know how Coyotes had such poison in their jaws. Maybe this was a new type, or maybe it was just his damned hallucinations. He just knew that whatever was inside of his blood wasn't supposed to be there and any poison would hurt him, that was certain. And after he was vulnerable due to the bite, infected with whatever was on the jaw of the Coyote, that's when they would come and drag him back to their den, where he would be immedi-ately eaten if he was lucky.

Jason wasn't going down without a fight. He had spent every single second in the wilderness fighting. He hadn't had a moment of peace since he had escaped.

Not. One. Single. Moment.

And he wasn't about to give up now.

When the coyote bit him, the bite felt strange. From the wound, he had been able to feel small, ice-cold tendrils creeping up his arm, leaving his nerves numb in its wake. The bite was different. It shot up his side, blazing hot, leaving every single nerve ending screaming in pain. Fumbling, he yanked the first aid kit out of his bag. There, in the same neat little row, Jason had first found them in, was five small syringes labeled the 'common' anti-venom. He pulled one from the kit and began to feel along his arm. He could feel his adrenaline-fueled pulse pounding against his fingertips. Carefully, he inserted the syringe into the artery and pushed down on the plunger. His face twisted in pain as the new foreign substance entered his body, but he continued to administer the drug. Once he emptied the entirety of the medicament into his bloodstream, he pulled out the syringe and tossed it aside. Then, he yanked off his lab coat. It was too dark to treat the bite mark itself, and he didn't have time to anyway. He did, however, need to staunch the blood flow as much as possible. He pushed the fabric against the wound and bound it tightly to his side with duct tape.

Jason stumbled to his feet, his mind racing. The Coyotes were waiting for the poison to take effect, he knew that. They would wait until he reached the paralysis or shock stage before attacking again. Only, that stage would never come for Jason (or so he hoped). The anti-venom had taken care of that. And, sooner or later, the Coyotes would figure out their bite wasn't working. They would attack again, only, this time, they wouldn't retreat. They would drag him away then and there, taking him back to whatever hell hole they crawled out of. He had a very limited amount of time to escape.

He pulled a small test tube out of his bag. After the various incidents that he'd had with grizzly bears, Jason only kept a limited amount of wolf pee on him, just in case he ran into some of the animals that he didn't want to run into. While he doubted it would completely cover up the scent of blood, it would buy him time. He yanked the cork out of the vial and splashed the pee over his body. Jason didn't think that bears were nocturnal hunters. And if they were, well, he'd take that predator over the other any day. At that thought, an idea struck him. An insane, suicidal idea that would probably get him killed in horrible and creative ways.

The Coyotes were the predators. Jason was the prey. And there was nothing he could do to change that fact.

But the Coyotes weren't the only predators in this area.

He slung his bag back over his shoulder. With his wolf claw in one hand and a flare in the other, Jason set out into the jungle.

He was an idiot. Hopefully, when this was over, he wouldn't be a dead idiot. The animals had finally figured out something was wrong. The prey wasn't reacting the way it was supposed to...

And now, they were actively hunting Jason.

A Coyote was near Jason. It was sniffing the air,

puzzled at why it couldn't smell him. Jason wasn't sure how long that would last, though. The wolf pee wouldn't hold it off forever. He just had to hope it would move on before discovering him. Currently, he was hidden behind a copse of trees, his hands tightly wrapped over his mouth to keep himself from screaming. He cautiously glanced around the wood. The Coyote was still there, making irritating growling sounds into the air. Jason quickly ducked back behind his feeble cover, pressing himself tightly against the trunk as he tried to quiet his shallow breaths. He was hyperaware of everything around him. He could feel the bark digging into his skin and see the trees rustling in the breeze and hear the same sounds of the country that had haunted him every single night. Only, this time, he was out with the noises. He had never truly been as exposed to Canada's nightlife as he was now. Even before he had found his truck, he still had a modicum of safety. He had spent those first few nights high in a tree, strapped in with his belt to keep from falling to the ground below. Never had he been on the forest floor, wounded and vulnerable.

Until now.

Slowly, he peeked around his cover again. The

Coyote was gone. He waited several long moments, searching for any sign of the animal, before cautiously leaving his hiding place. He needed to keep moving. Wolf territory was only about ten, fifteen minutes away if he took it at a dead run. He had made harder runs for the Cross-Country team at school.

Of course, back then he wasn't racing something that was trying to eat him. He could make it. He knew he could make it.

Something crashed into him at full speed. Jason hit the ground with a thud, all the air knocked out of him. The flare and claw skittered out of his hands. He struggled to his hands and knees and tried to crawl away, only to be tackled yet again. He and his attacker rolled across the rocky forest floor, coming to a stop a few feet away. Jason looked up at his assailant.

It was the first one he had seen. The same Coyote that had been searching for him before. The same one whose eye he had gouged out.

It had set a trap. And Jason had walked right into it. It crooned in victory, staring down at its prey. Jason was trapped beneath it, flat on his back, pinned down underneath the animal's weight. His hands scrambled uselessly at his sides, searching desperately for something to use as a weapon.

The animal reared back its head, its jaws open, ready to rip out his throat.

Jason's hands closed around a branch. The Coyote's head fell, its teeth descending closer and closer to his exposed flesh...

Only to clamp around the branch Jason had raised at the last moment as protection. Frustrated, the animal yanked its head free. Jason didn't waste a moment. He reared back his makeshift bludgeoning tool and slammed it into the beast's head. It stumbled off of him with a cry, wobbling as it walked. Jason struggled to his knees, raised the bat, and repeated the action. It jerked away, calling for its pack members to help.

Jason really, really didn't want to see what would happen when help arrived. He scrambled over to the site where he was tackled.

'They had to be here.' He needed the flare and claw; he wouldn't be able to get away without them. His hands passed uselessly through the dirt; he couldn't find anything in the darkness.

'Where were they?'

Jason could hear his followers and the predators coming closer and closer, the reinforcements apparently there.

'Where were they? Where were they?'

He wouldn't be able to outrun the Coyotes, Jason knew that. They were too fast, and he was injured. He needs the flare to make them shy away.

'Where were they? Where were they? Where were they?'

The animals were closing in.

'Where were they? Where were they? Where were they? Where were they?'

He saw the flare. It was lying a few feet away next to the wolf claw. He dove forward, grabbing the flare and ripping open the top.

Nothing happened.

Jason's heart stopped.

Then, the torch sparked to life, casting a red glow on the surrounding area as it sizzled in his hand. Jason spun around, thrusting it in the face of the nearest animal. It jerked back with a scream and a howl, its eyes suffering from the sudden glare. Jason grabbed the claw with his free hand and staggered to his feet. He waved the light in a wide arc around him, illuminating the carnivores surrounding him. There were four of them, all of which retreated with a cry. They stumbled off into the jungle, letting loose calls for help.

Jason turned around and ran in the opposite direction. It wasn't over; they wouldn't let their prey slip away so easily. The Coyotes would be back, only, next time, they'd have much more support. He sprinted towards wolf territory, the flare still burning in his hand.

The hunt was on, again. And hopefully, for the final time. But he knew that he wouldn't last long. He was already bitten, injured and extremely tired due to the adrenaline and the pure and utter danger he was feeling inside of his body. He knew that he had to do something about all this before it all came crashing down upon him and he had to work before things went bad, really bad.

So, Jason ran, and he knew the Coyotes followed. They wanted him and, one way or another, they would have him. The only thing was, they would kill him if he was caught, there would be no escape this time around. He had to run, and run, and run and run as fast as he could. And he was going to run as fast as he could, as fast as his legs could carry. He knew that he had to run. And just as he snapped out of the bushes and the forests, he saw the large barriers of the Canadian/American border. And his heart stopped.

He had made it. He had made it to the border, he had made it as CLOSE to his home as he could get, he had made it and there was no other way to explain this. He was home, he was home, he was home.

And right as he was celebrating inside of his head, a Coyote jumped on top of him again, pinning him against the ground. And that is when he realized he was done for. This time, he wouldn't live. He could feel the animal's breath on his skin and he could feel the way it breathed down upon him, its claws ready to tear him out.

Jason planned to lure it into the wolf territory, and it

hadn't worked as he had gone in the wrong direction. Perhaps the wolves lived in some other area of the forest? Either way, he had ended up near the border, and now all he had to do was follow it until he reached some patrol and he would be free. But he wasn't free, not now. He was captured, and he was about to die.

'I'm sorry, mum, I couldn't make it.' He said his last prayers. 'I am sorry, Dad, I never became a soccer player. I am sorry, Rax, I was never able to be your best man at your wedding. I am sorry, Selene, I never could ask you out and I am sorry, Grandfather, I wasn't strong enough. Perhaps you can whoop me when I meet you.'

But the pain and the agony and the cold hand of death never came. Instead, what came was the sound of a gun being loaded, and shot right at the Coyote on top of him. Jason's eyes widened as he looked up from where the gunshot had come from, or the gunshots, apparently.

The Coyotes were howling and running, trying to escape, but they were quickly shot down as harshly as they could be. There were no wildlife members to stop them this time, as this was the Canadian

National Army. All of the Army members were wearing their green and dark green camo-suits, with their gear on, and all of them were apparently looking at him strangely. Jason was, for a moment, thinking he was dead as if he was in some sick dream. There was no way this was real, right? Like, there was no way that this was actually happening, right? No, this wasn't possible. And that is when all changed when one of them came to him and helped him up. The pain of the bite he had suffered from the cuts he had on him and the survival he had done was bright inside of his head and body. He looked at the man wondrously, a pale-skinned handsome man.

"Are you Jason Smith of New York?" The man asked him in a Canadian accent. All of the other army-members were looking around them, in the dull of the morning light. "The one that made the distress call?"

"Y-yes." Jason nodded, stuttering. "Yes, I am. I am Jason Smith from New York."

"Mr. Smith, I am Colonel James Exton. This is my team." The man introduced himself. "We are sorry if we were late, we just couldn't find a safe way to come to the place, and we had to drive down last night. It took a long time to confirm that you were truly telling the truth. We found the place where the Kidnappers were hiding and we also found the Nabbers, they still hadn't left, afraid that they would be killed by the wildlife. We also found the water truck that you lived in, the military bunker, and followed your path on one of the maps. We saw the flare and it was lucky that we found you."

"W-What do you mean?" Jason was in shock. "Y-you are... you are actually?"

"Yes, sir. We are here to rescue you and bring you home." The man smiled as a jeep suddenly came from behind them. Four of them. "We are your rescue party, and for surviving the wildlife of Canada, we salute you, sir."

And at once, all of them saluted him, and for Jason, it all felt like a dream. Jason nodded and shakily saluted them back, tears already falling from his eyes. Without warning, he hugged the Colonel who didn't look shocked at all. Instead, he only pulled him in, like he was expecting to.

"Thank you." Jason cried hard. He had previously cried for all he had lost and all he had gone through.

But this time, he cried because he was safe. Because he was rescued. Because he had survived.

"Please, let our medic look over you first," James said as he let Jason go, and pointed him towards a man waiting for him with his medical bags. "And till then, we will inform everyone that we found you."

But Jason didn't care.

He had survived.

He had lived.

He was strong.

And he was never, ever going to give up.

CHAPTER FOUR

In the end, Jason Smith was taken to Vancouver so he could go through some heavy observations. He had several infections, had mistakenly taken an anti-venom due to hallucinations from the loss of electrolytes, and he had also not had a proper meal for weeks.

Even before Jason had arrived there, his parents were waiting for him, and Jason had never cried as much as he had when in his mother's tearful and tight embrace. He was a sight to see, his long hair, matted due to the dirt, his body littered with scars and his eyes having a haunted look in them.

When Jason returned to America, he was greeted like a hero; greeted like someone that had not only survived the wild but someone that had survived the war. He was greeted by Rax with the biggest bear-hug he could give, by Selene with the largest kiss that he could get and by his other friends and family members with the biggest cheer he could receive. And only when he was home did he realize what had happened.

The kidnappers took him because of his father. They thought they would get large amounts of money out of his father who was a CEO for a tech company. But Jason had survived, he had escaped, he had lived and made it back home. His kidnappers were all US nationals and were facing harsh penalties for the crimes they committed.

And as for Jason? He was never going to forget the wildlife, he was never going to forget the thrill of survival and the fear of death. So, it was no surprise that when he graduated from high school, he chose the career of joining the military and being a marine. Jason was a true survivor.

THE END